REBELS

102900 862118 000012   GHOST SHIP   001036 10

STAR WARS

Rebel Faction

OUTODO 11 10

010

3

STAR WARS REBELS™

TIE FIGHTER
TROUBLE

Based on the episode "Fighter Fight,"
written by Kevin Hopps

Adapted by Brooke Vitale

© & TM 2014 Lucasfilm Ltd.

Published by Disney • Lucasfilm Press, an imprint of Disney Book Group. No part of this book may be reproduced or transmitted in any form or by any means, electronic or mechanical, including photocopying, recording, or by any information storage and retrieval system, without written permission from the publisher. For information address Disney • Lucasfilm Press, 1101 Flower Street, Glendale, California 91201.

Printed in China
First Edition, December 2014
1 3 5 7 9 10 8 6 4 2

ISBN 978-1-4847-2610-5
T425-2382-5-14356

Visit the official *Star Wars* website at: www.starwars.com
This book was printed on paper created from a sustainable source.

Disney
LUCASFILM
P R E S S

Los Angeles • New York

"Okay, you can do this," Ezra told himself. Focusing all his energy, he tried to use the Force to lift a bowl of cereal.

Suddenly, the bowl rose into the air. Ezra couldn't believe he had done it! Then he noticed that Chopper was holding up the bowl.

"Chopper!" Ezra shouted angrily as the droid sped away. "Come back here, you rolling junk pile."

Ezra chased Chopper into his bedroom, where Zeb was trying to sleep. All their noise woke the tired Lasat.

"I'm crushing you both," Zeb said angrily.

Ezra raced from the room with Zeb close on his heels.

The pair crashed into a pile of crates and barrels that Kanan had just finished stacking.

When Hera saw the mess, she was furious. She sent Ezra and Zeb on a supply run to get them off the ship. "Don't even think about coming back without at least one meiloorun fruit. Clear?"

Ezra and Zeb nodded and trudged off to find the supplies on the list.

"How do you expect them to find meiloorun on Lothal?" Kanan asked when they were gone.

Hera smiled. Ezra and Zeb didn't need to know that they'd been sent on a wild-goose chase!

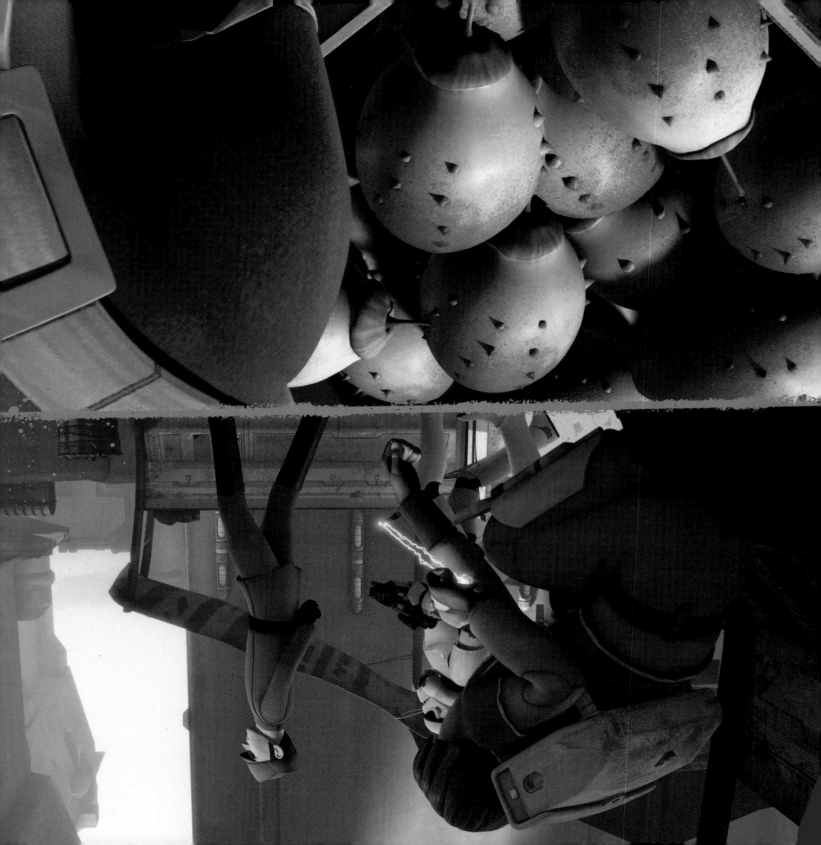

At the Kothal marketplace, Zeb and Ezra decided to split up to find supplies. Ezra was looking for meiloorun when he spotted an old friend, Morad Sumar.

Ezra asked Sumar if he had any of the special fruits, but Sumar just laughed. "Meilooruns don't grow on Lothal," he told the boy.

Feeling sheepish, Ezra waved good-bye to Sumar. He was just starting to walk away when he saw an Imperial supply master heading toward him. Ezra quickly ducked behind a stand, but the supply master didn't want him. He was coming for Sumar. He wanted to buy Sumar's farm for the Empire, but Sumar refused to sell.

When the supply master left, Ezra stepped out from behind the stand. He bumped into Zeb—and a crate of meilooruns!

"How much for the whole crate?" Zeb asked the owner of the stand.

But the crate was already sold. As Ezra watched, two stormtroopers picked it up and loaded it onto a cargo transport. He wasn't going to give up so easily.

Ezra waited for the troopers to turn their backs. Then he slipped around the transport and hopped aboard.

Ezra had just opened the crate and pulled out a meiloorun when a trooper spotted him.

At the same time, Zeb threw his crate of supplies at the trooper. "Run!" he cried.

Zeb and Ezra took off, but the two were quickly separated.

Zeb raced down an abandoned alley and found an empty
TIE fighter. He quickly climbed inside.

Elsewhere in the marketplace, several troopers chased Ezra from roof to roof.

Ezra fired his slingshot over his shoulder, but the stun-balls just bounced off the troopers.

Just then, a TIE fighter rose up next to him. "Great . . . Just what I need," Ezra muttered.

Ezra looked at the fighter. Was that *Zeb* inside?

"Zeb? Zeb, let me in!" he called.

Zeb opened the canopy and Ezra jumped inside. But the cockpit wasn't meant to hold two people.

"Keep your elbows off the controls!" Zeb shouted.

"You couldn't find something a little roomier?" Ezra asked.

The two were so busy arguing that they didn't notice they were headed right for the cargo transport.

On the ground, the troopers saw the TIE fighter coming their way and ducked.

CRASH! The fighter smashed through the crate of meilooruns and back up into the air.

Zeb looked at the windshield. It was covered in splattered meilooruns.

"I can't see anything," he said.

Ezra closed his eyes. Using the Force, he grabbed the control stick and pulled. The TIE fighter swerved, just avoiding a building.

Safe from the stormtroopers, Zeb and Ezra called the *Ghost*. Kanan was not happy that they had stolen a TIE fighter. He ordered them to fly back to the *Ghost* right away.

Meanwhile, on the ground, the Imperial supply master had gone to see Sumar at his farm.

"I told you before, we're not selling," Sumar said.

"You misunderstand," the supply master said. "We are no longer interested in buying."

And with that, he ordered his men to set fire to the farm.

High above, Ezra saw the smoke. "I think I know where it's coming from," he told Zeb. "Go check it out. Please."

Zeb turned the fighter. Soon they reached the burning farmhouse. Several transports were driving away from it.

"Friends of yours?" Zeb asked Ezra.

"Of my parents," Ezra replied.

Zeb sighed. "We're going in, aren't we?"

Ezra nodded. "Just get me in close."

Zeb carefully piloted the TIE fighter close to a transport. Ezra swung down and saw where Sumar and his wife were being held prisoner.

"Hold on. I'll have you out soon!" he told them.

Ezra stretched out his arm, but he couldn't quite reach the transport's control panel. Squeezing his eyes tight, he reached out with his mind. *Click.* The prisoners' shackles opened.

As the prisoners ran away, stormtroopers opened fire on Ezra.

Ezra leaped into another transport. Ducking behind a crate, he saw something. One meiloorun had survived the crash!

Ezra tucked the fruit under his arm and climbed on top of the transport. Zeb flew down and pulled him inside the TIE fighter.

Back at the *Ghost*, Zeb handed Hera the piece of fruit.

"Forget about the fruit," Kanan yelled. "Where's the TIE fighter?"

"I crashed it!" Zeb said.

Ezra grinned. "After all, we didn't want it to fall into enemy hands."

Zeb patted Ezra on the back. Then, side by side, the two friends headed to their room for a well-deserved rest.